10 Year Old Ricco Gonzales

And

The Big Cats on Panther Mountain

Ricco Gonzales had lost his mother and father to the jungle when he was just a baby. He now lives with his old grandfather in a small grass hut near the village of Matoon, which lies deep in the Brazilian jungle.

This village sits not only at the base of Panther Mountain so named for the dreadful killer cats that live there, but also at the very edge of the mysterious Black Forest, known to all who live there as the jungle of fear!

Grandfather has lived in this village all his life and every day since he was a young boy has made his way up the mountain to tend his coffee bean plants. It is dangerous to be on the mountain any time but less so if one is careful and travels only in the daytime. The work of harvesting the beans can be done without fear of falling prey to the terrible animal that has taken so many lives of those who did not heed the warning of the mountain. For the big cat walks the mountain at night and those unsuspecting will surely fall prey to its powerful jaws.

There was no hiding from the panther, if in a cave he would sniff you out. If in a tree he would climb and get you. Anyone who returned to the village after spending the night on the mountain was considered to have special powers. In all the year's grandfather could remember there had only been one person that had done that. Ramona Gabriela had returned from a night on the mountain and told of turning herself into a Raven and flying away at the very instant the big cat was about to grab her.

Of course grandfather didn't believe all of that. He would scoff and say, "she was just lucky Ricco, the nearest she ever comes to a Raven is when they try and steal food out of her basket". "No one turns into a bird Ricco, not even that ugly old woman". Then he would laugh and say, "Of course it might not be such a bad idea at that". "It would make it a lot easier for her to get up the mountain every day". He would spread his arms and make like a flying bird and Ricco would laugh at his old grandfather.

Ricco's mother and father had fallen prey to the terrible panther and he was injured as well and it is he who must now always walk with a crutch. His leg is now stiff from the hip down and he must swing it in the direction he wants to go. He had grown with his disability and had learned to adjust to the difference between himself and the rest of the children in the village. He moves slowly and must be careful where he places his bad foot or else he will fall and when that happens it takes a long time to get back up and get going again.

Grandfather stood over Ricco's bed listening as Ricco told him he would rather sleep later this morning. "I will stay in bed this morning grandfather, there is no need to go to the mountain this morning the plants will be fine without me."

"Not this morning Ricco, this morning you must eat your biscuit on the way. There is much work to do and you know we must be off the mountain before dark. Now come, come, hurry it is time to go".

Although it was early, the day was already hot, and it was a two hour walk up the steep mountain path to where grandfather's coffee plants were. The going was slow and grandfather leaned on his hoe handle with each step. Occasionally he would turn looking back down the path to be sure they were not being followed by one of the dreaded mountain cats.

"What would you do if you saw him grandfather? You could not stop the panther. He would just eat us both. Then who would harvest the beans"?

"Ah, grandson, that old cat knows my smell. He has watched me for years. I do not believe he would eat me even if he had the chance. I'm now too old for his taste". Grandfather made his eyes big and leaning over he looked at Ricco. "You, on the other hand are young and tender. What a meal you would make young man!" He felt Ricco's arm and nodded. "Oh yes, he would like you very much".

Glancing back down the trail Ricco began walking more quickly. "Hurry up grandfather we have much work to do before dark. How can we get our work done if we stand and talk all day"?

Grandfather laughed and started back up the path that led to their mountain garden. It was still quite early in the morning when they arrived, and after eating another biscuit they began their days work on the coffee plants. There was much to do with the pruning and pulling of the weeds away from around the bottom of the plants so the rains would give them plenty of water.

It was not necessary for Ricco to use his crutch while working because he could hold on to the plants for balance if needed. Leaning his crutch up against one of the plants he started work. Pruning the plants and checking the beans for ripeness. Grandfather had taught him well and he was very good at his work.

The day passed quickly and as the sun was starting to set grandfather and Ricco prepared to start back down the mountain. Picking up the leather bag and the hoe used for weeding together they started back down the path toward the village.

"It was a good days work grandson. Your leg does not seem to bother you much when you are working.

I am glad to see that. Someday these plants will be all yours to work and care for. Then you can teach your son as I have taught you and as my father taught me".

Ricco smiled at grandfather and dreamed of one day selling many beans and living in a fine house in the city. But then he would have to leave his village and his coffee bean plants and worst of all his grandfather. "No" he decided. "I will stay right here and live in the village".

Suddenly grandfather yelled in pain! Ricco hurried to the old man's side and saw that he had caught his foot in a root that had grown up into the path, and had fallen. He was holding his leg just above the ankle and grimacing in pain. "Ricco, I believe I have broken my ankle. It will be dark soon and you must help me up so we can get off the mountain before dark. The big cats will be walking these paths soon and we must not be here then".

The old man put his arm around Ricco's shoulder and after several tries they were able to get grandfather to his feet. It was of no use however. With Ricco's bad leg and grandfathers hurt leg even together they could not walk and after just a very few steps Ricco lowered grandfather back down to the ground.

Together they were able to get grandfather leaned back up against a tree and then Ricco sat down beside him. In silence they watched as the sun began to set behind the mountain and almost to the second after the sun was down the scream of the big mountain cat could be heard in the distance. Both of them knew that if one would but look in the morning the cats footprints would be seen on this very path.

"Grandfather, we must get down the mountain or we will surly perish! The panther will surly come this way. We must try again to move you. Come! Let me help you up again".

The old man was tired from his days work and his leg hurt very badly. Shaking his head no, he would not look at Ricco. When he spoke Ricco had to lean over and hold his ear close to the old man's mouth to hear him.

"Grandson, I love you very much and I can go no further and you must now leave me and try to get off this mountain".

Ricco drew back in horror! "No, grandfather! I will not leave you here to die! I love you and I will not leave you"! The old man shrugged his shoulders and spread his hands in defeat. "It does not matter Ricco, I have lived a long time and if you are not here who will tend the plants? Go now and save yourself. As it is you will be fortunate to get off this mountain alive. Now go, Ricco, go"!

The ten year old looked at his grandfather, stood up and without saying a word walked off into the darkness of the mountain. The old man watched him go and with tears in his eyes leaned back against the tree to await his fate. The big cats scream could once again be heard in the distance and grandfather could tell it was closer than before. His last thought before falling asleep from the pain in his leg was of his grandson standing in the sun outside their hut in the village.

As soon as Ricco left he began looking for something he had been thinking about while grandfather had been telling him to leave. Alongside the path that led down the mountain was a stream that supplied the village with water and trees lined either side of the stream and for many years had been the source of firewood whenever grandfather needed to build a fire. Between his crutch and the steep mountain path Ricco had a hard time with the wood. He could only carry one piece at a time and as he placed each piece on the ground in front of the old man he became more determined than ever to save him. He did not know how a boy of ten would fight off a mountain cat and save grandfather but he would try. He could not imagine living without the old man. With his bad leg he could not move as fast as he would like, but right now, in this place, he had to overcome the problem and do what he must. His thoughts were interrupted by the ever closer scream of the panther and Ricco knew the big cat would soon smell his prey. He knew he must hurry.

It seemed to take forever, but after many trips the pile of wood was now in place. He had set a few pieces aside to replace the ones that burned away. Putting dry grass under some of the smaller pieces he reached for his flint and after a few strokes managed to get a fire going. As it began to blaze the smoke increased and began to drift along the side of the mountain.

As big cats go this one was very big. Having been born on this mountain several years ago it had never left. The destruction he had caused over the years had been great. More than once he had caught an unsuspecting traveler alone on this path at night and done his terrible work. Used to the taste of human blood he had known many easy kills and just now as he smelled the smoke he knew that humans would be near. Ever so silently he started in that direction. The monsoon season was now upon them and the dark threatening clouds blocked out the moonlight all the way to the horizon. It mattered not to this big cat for his nose told him all he needed to know. His every step was taking him closer and closer to Ricco and grandfather.

As Ricco sat looking into the night sky he could hear the thunder and see the lightning off into the distance. He prayed the rain would hold off at least until daylight so he could somehow get grandfather off the mountain. The fire began to hiss at about the same time he felt the first raindrops on his face. Soon the fire was nothing more than wet smoldering wood, and he and grandfather now found they were in total darkness. Ricco was now frightened for grandfather and himself. Lowering his head to his knees he began to silently cry.

The big cat was now not more than a short distance away. The smoke had stopped, but it made no difference. Smelling his prey he slowed his approach and began to sniff the night air. Soon, he would sort out all the smells and follow the right one directly to Grandfather and Ricco. Many times before he had done this and he knew there was no hurry. This was his mountain and no one ever escaped. Lowering his head he became very intent on what he was doing. The big panther made no sound as he moved along through the darkness and in just a short time would surprise his prey.

The hair on the back of Ricco's neck stood up causing him to jerk his head around and stare out into the darkness. Lightning flashed and he made a decision. "He is coming. The panther is coming! I must move grandfather further back off the path". Looking around desperately for someplace else to hide he could almost smell the rain soaked fur of the big cat. He was near, very near to grandfather and Ricco. If he didn't move quickly it would be too late for the both of them. Then he saw it! Not twenty feet away was a dead fall. A huge tree that had been blown down in a storm. The center had long ago been hollowed out by wood ants, and it might just be big enough to hide him and grandfather from the big cat.

Shaking the old man by the shoulders he tried to wake him up. "Grandfather! Wake up! He is coming! Grandfather! Grandfather!" it was no use the old man had fainted from the pain in his ankle and would not wake up!

Throwing down his crutch he grabbed the old man by his feet and balancing himself as best he could on his good leg he pulled with all his strength toward the downed tree. It was no use! He had not moved grandfather one inch. Determined to save the old man he forced himself to put weight on his bad leg. The pain was very bad, but now it mattered not. He was going to save grandfather from the big cat and was going to do whatever was necessary to do that. Pulling again grandfather moved ever so slightly. Ricco then knew he could do it. "Yes! Grandfather yes! We will beat the big cat! He will not eat you or me". The ground was now very wet from the rain and when Ricco pulled again grandfather began to slide slowly along toward the tree. In just a few minutes he and grandfather were there at the fallen tree.

The thunder and lightning was terrible indeed. Lightning hit very hard on the side of the mountain scaring Ricco something awful, but the flashes gave him enough light to allow him to see what he was doing. Reaching the base of the tree he reached under grandfathers arms and locked his hands around the old man's chest. Pulling him to his feet Ricco forced him into the hole the wood ants had made in the old tree. Hurrying back to get his crutch he climbed into the hole himself and pushed grandfather as far back into the hollowed out tree as possible. He could still see out but at least they were now off the ground. When the panther came he would just have to do the best he could.

The hoe! He had forgotten the hoe! If the panther smelled the hoe he would jump up into the tree and eat them both! Just then the lightning flashed and he could see the hoe leaning up against the tree where grandfather had been sitting. Jumping down from the tree Ricco started across the small space separating him from the hoe. Reaching the spot he picked up the hoe just as the big cat screamed again.

REEOWRRR! Ricco froze in his tracks. The panther was close, very close, it could not be more than a few hundred feet away at most. If he didn't hurry it would be too late. In that moment he forgot all about the pain in his leg and began moving very quickly across the clearing toward the tree. Tossing the hoe into the tree he climbed in after it and settled himself as far back into the tree as he could and waited.

The driving rain had somewhat dulled the panther's sense of smell and he neither heard no could smell exactly where Ricco was. He became angry and the scream Ricco heard was the big cat letting out his anger. Had the night been a clear or even a quiet one, Ricco and grandfather would have been no more. As it was he was able to reach the tree and hide as best he could.

Grandfather woke up shortly after Ricco had gone after the hoe and heard the big cat scream. He was very relieved when Ricco climbed back into the tree. Both of them sat huddled together and stared out into the night. Another flash of lightning hit very hard on the mountain and they looked on in terror at the very spot where grandfather had been leaning up against the tree. In that flash of light there was a clear view of the cat outlined against the mountain, he must have been at least eight feet from nose to tail and was as black as coal.

His eyes shone like white hot coals in the light of the storm. Lightning flashed again and he was gone. It was right about then that Ricco found it hard to breathe. It wasn't until grandfather put his hand on his shoulder that he began to calm down some. There was no telling just where the big cat was and even though he sat holding the hoe ready to defend grandfather he knew he would be no match for the panther should he find them. Nevertheless he held the hoe very tightly and dare not breathe.

REEOWRRR the scream came again and Ricco realized the panther was sitting just above his head on the very tree they were hiding in! He was so frightened he covered his face with his hands. He dare not look for he knew that in the next instant the panther would leap into the tree and he didn't want to think about what was about to happen to him and grandfather.

The storm raged all night and it seemed he had been sitting that way forever. When he finally pulled his hands away from his face and looked out he could see the night sky was finally giving way to the dawn, and it had stopped raining. Grandfather leaned forward and whispered in Ricco's ear.

"Grandson, the rain has washed away our smell and the evil one could not find us. Come, we must go now and get off this mountain. That panther will be very angry because he couldn't fine us. You are brave indeed Ricco. You were willing to stay and fight the panther to save your old grandfather. Wait! Wait until I tell the village! Oh how brave you are"!

Ricco smiled at grandfather. "I was not brave grandfather. I was very frightened. I could hardly breathe. How can we get you off this mountain this morning if we couldn't get you off last night"?

"Ah, but grandson you forget I am this morning in the presence of a very brave man. Come, we will find a way".

Ricco took a tree branch and made a crutch that looked much like his own for grandfather, and together they walked down of the mountain and into the village. Grandfather's ankle healed and they spent many more years working on the coffee plants together always being careful to be off the mountain before dark. At night the panther's scream could be heard up on the mountain as he looked for those who had escaped him, and many times when Ricco would arrive to tend the plants, he would find the footprints left by the big cat as it had looked for him.

Ricco stood a little taller because he knew he had beaten the killer of the mountain at his own game. He had been able to do so because he hadn't given in to his "difference", but had accepted the challenge and through determination had won the battle.

Grandfather is gone now and Ricco's days are spent teaching his own son how to tend the plants that sit high up on Panther Mountain. Every once in a while, he can be heard telling of the night he and grandfather had spent on the mountain. The story hasn't changed much over the years, but the lesson he learned has made him add a line or two. A line or two we might all consider.

This is what Grandfather has taught us all.

"My son, you must always remember, even if others see you as different, others are seen by you as different also. Even when there are differences, we are all men and women, and all are equal. If you want to do a thing badly enough, you can do it. No matter how difficult it may seem at the time".

The Twins

If you were to ride the wings of the eagle and follow the sun not too far a distance, you would come upon a strange and wonderful place. Here is where the morning sun shines down through the trees and warms the ferns on the floor of what is called the enchanted forest. This is the place where the morning birds sing such lovely melodies, and rabbits scurry here and there and the streams run gently toward the sea through this land of rainbows and waterfalls.

At the outer edge of this beautiful place there sits a small cottage with two little windows and a crooked little chimney. Here is where a little girl and boy of six or so live with their mama and papa. Their names are Luke and Yelena Stillgrin. Their family is very poor, but it doesn't matter for they love each other very much. Mama Stillgrin has her garden and Papa Stillgrin milks the cow and gathers the eggs from the chickens and trades them in town for the things they need,

Luke and Yelena are very nice children, it does not matter to them that their clothes are patched or their coats are made from rags Mama Stillgrin found behind the tailors shop in the village. They are warm on cold winter days and their smiles are always bright and cheery. Luke and Yelena are like the other boys and girls who live in this part of the world, but with them there is a difference. You see, shortly after the twins were born a very bad sickness took away their sight and although they grew and were very healthy in every way their lack of sight made them different. Many days the children of the village would try and play with Luke and Yelena, but they could not kick a ball they could not see, or chase a butterfly, or see the Blue Bird, or follow the rainbow. Sometimes when they would try and play with the other children they would bump into things and it would hurt so badly they would just sit right down and cry. The other children would feel bad and try to help, but it was no use, because Like and Yelena were just not like them. The two would go home and ask their Mama and Papa, "Why are we not like the other children? Will we always have to be in one place? Will we never be able to go and play like the other children"? Mama and Papa Stillgrin would feel very bad for them not only because they were not like the other children, but they were afraid for them too. Mama would always give them a big hug and say "You must stay right here because if you were to wander off we would never see you again, Mama and Papa will be right here to take care of you". So Luke and Yelena would spend their days sitting on the stoop in front of the little cottage and listening to the sounds around them.

Onc bright morning Mama got the two of them ready to go outdoors putting their warm coat of rags on them, and their stocking caps she had knitted and their little mittens. When she had sat them down on the stoop Mama patted their little heads and said, "You stay right here and if you want anything you call Mama".

As Luke and Yelena sat there they could hear all the sounds of the world around them. Off in the distance they could hear the sounds of the children playing in the village and behind them they could hear the peaceful and wonderful sounds of the forest. Suddenly a big smile came across Luke's face! "Yelena" he said "Today we are going to go exploring". Reaching over by the door he picked up the walking sticks Papa Stillgrin had made for them and reaching over he took hold of his sisters hand and they stepped off the step and carefully began working their way around the side of the cottage toward Mama's garden. In just a few minutes they had passed Mama's garden and had disappeared into the forest.

Very carefully they walked touching the ground in front of them with their little walking sticks. When they would touch something on the forest floor they would carefully step over it and go on. Every so often they would stop and listen to the sounds around them and breathe in the wonderful smells of the forest. Their world was dark, but they would imagine what each sound looked like and it was new and exciting for them.

The twins didn't know it, but the animals of the forest stood by ever so quietly as these little blind children walked past them. "Oh, how wonderful "Yelena thought as they walked along. She could smell the freshness of the things around her and hear the birds singing in the trees above. The wet ferns growing on the forest floor gently brushed her fingertips that tasted sweet and made little Yelena smile.

On and on they walked until their little legs got so tired they had to sit down on the forest floor to rest. It wasn't long before they were fast asleep and as they lay sleeping the animals one by one began to come very close to look at them. First to come was the Raccoon, then the Fox, and the Rabbit, and the Deer, and then the Bear, until a great many of the animals who lived in the forest were gathered around them on this dark and lonely night. Curious at first, as time passed they too became tired and sleepy, until finally the only one watching over them was the old Hoot Owl sitting high up in the tree above them.

After several hours Luke woke up and waking his sister and said, "We better start home now Mama and Papa will be worried about us". Yelena stretched her arms and stood up. "Yes we have been gone a very long time". Picking up their walking sticks they started out, but unbeknown to them they were walking in the wrong direction. Deeper and deeper into the forest they walked each step taking them further and further from home, they walked past the Fox, and the Bear, past the Deer, and the Wolf, past the Rabbit, and the Porcupine. All the animals knew the children weren't afraid of them and as they walked they wondered "Who are these little ones that walk among us showing no fear? They must be very special". And indeed they were very special.

The twins were now very deep into the forest and were now very hungry and tired. This time when they sat down to rest they were a very frightened little boy and girl. With tears running out of their big brown eyes they called out into the darkness. "Mama, Papa". But there was no answer. Through tears they called out again and again, "Mama, Papa". But the only sound they heard that night was the old Hoot Owl that once again rested in the branches above them.

"We are lost" Yelena said at last "We are all alone and will never see Mama and Papa again". She began to cry, then Luke began to cry too, but they were not alone. Had they been able they would have seen all the animals that had been walking along with them that were now sitting in a circle around them. They knew this little girl and boy were lost and they had been crying too.

When Luke and Yelena finally were asleep Mr. Bear spoke ever so softly. "These little ones are lost and we must help them get back home. I do not believe they even know we are here, because they cannot see, so it is up to us to take care of them. Mr. Raccoon you must move things from their path as they walk, and Deer you must scout the way. Mr. Fox you must go and find Redbone and bring her back here as fast as you can. The rest of you will come along and help. Now you had better all get some sleep while I stand guard, I'm afraid it is going to be a very long night".

Mr. Fox took off running lickety split. Using every short cut and secret path he knew that would get him to where Redbone lived. It took some time, but finally he was there. Walking very carefully past the hen house and the barn so as not to wake anyone. Redbone saw him coming and raised her head.

"What is it Mr. Fox? What brings you here on this dark night"?

"Redbone thank heavens you are here, Bear sent me. You must come quickly. There is a little blind boy and girl lost in the woods. We need you to help get them home. I believe they live near the village on the other side of the forest. Come, we must hurry"!

Redbone was on her feet and running toward the forest before Mr. Fox had finished talking. "Lead the way Mr. Fox and don't worry about showing me your shortcuts I already know them all, just get me to the children".

Redbone and Mr. Fox were running side by side working their way deeper and deeper into the forest where Luke and Yelena lay sleeping among all the animals. When they arrived Redbone sat and listened while Mr. Bear filled her in on what had happened. Walking over she lay down between Luke and Yelena and gently laid her head on Yelena's leg and looked at her. "You mean these children can't see? How in the world did they ever get this deep into the forest?

Never mind, let them sleep, when they wake we will take them home. They are beautiful aren't they"? When Yelena woke up she felt something very heavy on her leg. "Oh" she cried and tried to move away but she couldn't it was just too heavy. Luke woke up as well and reached out his hand and felt a very big warm nose. Moving his hand up, he felt a very big and head and long ears. "It's alright Yelena I think it is just an animal of the forest that has come to keep us warm. I do not think it will hurt us". With his hand resting on Redbones head he and his sister went back to sleep not knowing they had many friends there with them.

The morning sun shining down through the trees warmed the twins waking them up. Luke stretched and said "I am very hungry we must hurry home so Mama can fix us something to eat. Feeling for their walking sticks Luke and Yelena stood up and started out again. The children took one step and ran right into something very big and soft and warm. With both hands they felt Redbone. There was the same big head, long ears, and warm nose, but this time there was something else. A big tongue wet on their faces they laughed and together gave Redbone a hug. Once again they started out, but this time they felt the big animal walking between them. Luke and Yelena laid a hand on Redbones back and held on as they walked along. Redbone looked over at Bear and he nodded his approval. The other animals scurried here and there working their way around the twins and Redbone. Deer was out in front making sure the path was safe for the two children and Raccoon hurried along in front of them making sure anything that might make them fall was removed.

All the animals were busy protecting Luke and Yelena as they walked along through the enchanted forest on that beautiful morning. Together they crossed small brooks and went through sun brightened clearings and one time they all walked right through the end of a beautiful rainbow.

The twins had walked for a long time lost and it was a very long way back to their little cottage at the edge of the forest. Three times they lay down and slept always with their hands on that big warm head of Redbone. The animals were always around them with Mr. Bear standing guard of course.

Poor Mama and Papa were very worried and had been searching everywhere for Luke and Yelena, but not finding them had all but given up. They had heard of others going into the enchanted forest and never being heard of again. With tears in her eyes Mama Stillgrin opened the door of the little cottage for the third day ready to call out for the children and to her surprise there they were! Standing right in front of the cottage were Luke and Yelena and standing right beside them was their friend with the big warm head. It was a Redbone Hound!

Mama Stillgrin screamed for Papa. 'Papa, our little Luke and Yelena are home!' Papa Stillgrin came to the door and when he saw the children standing with the hound he knew they were just fine.

Most hounds love children and this hound in particular wouldn't let anything happen to this special little boy and girl. Besides there were all the other animals of the forest stand just out of sight at the edge of the forest.

While watching over Luke and Yelena all these days they too had come to love them. After all the whole bunch had walked through the end of a rainbow hadn't they?

From that time on Yelena and Luke could go anywhere they wished. They would just lay their hands on Redbone's back and she would take them wherever they wanted to go. Never again did they have to sit out in front of the cottage.

What of the other animals that helped the children? Well sometimes Redbone will take a turn and walk them right back into the enchanted forest to meet them. There are lots of hugs and they all walk quietly along past the beautiful waterfalls, and through the rainbows. In that special place with a Redbone Hound by their side who knows what a boy or girl of six or so can see?

What we learned.

If you watch real close you might just see a little or even a big person walking along holding to a dog. You see they don't have to sit out in front of their cottage's anymore either.

☺

Jeremy, and the Goose

There is a place in the land of dreams, just beyond the shadow of the eastern mountains. Where the land rolls gently and the meadows are filled with beautiful flowers, marshes and lily ponds.

It was in a place such as this that a little boy of six or so once lived. His name was Jeremy Kind.

Jeremy was like all the other little boys and girls that lived in this beautiful place except for two things. When Jeremy was born, he could neither speak nor hear like the other boys and girls.

Jeremy lived with his mother and father in a little cottage just outside the village that lay just beyond the shadow of the mountain.

When Jeremy was little and played by himself, he did not know he was any different from the other children. Then one day he discovered he was the only person in the land there about that could not speak or hear.

Sometimes when Jeremy would play with the other little boys and girls and they could not understand him, he would become very sad and would go and sit all by himself.

His world was very quiet, but he did not really mind very much. Jeremy began to see the beauty of the mountains and the meadows where he lived. It was very easy to pay attention to what he was doing when there was no noise to bother him.

He was a kind and gentle little boy with bright eyes and a beautiful smile.

One bright and sunny day Jeremy was exploring along the path that ran just behind his little cottage. He had never been this way before, and after walking just a short way, came upon a clearing with a beautiful lily pond.

His little eyes brightened and his face broke into a big smile. Because right out there on that lily pond, swam a giant gander and seven beautiful geese.

He could also see some of the children from the village were on the other side of the pond. He slipped behind a nearby tree and watched as some of the children tried to coax the big birds to the bank. They would throw crumbs of bread out on the water and the geese wanting to eat it, would start to swim closer to the bank. Each time the big gander would swim in front of them and head them back into the middle of the pond. Jeremy watched as the gander placed himself between the children and the other geese. He understood it was the ganders' way of keeping the other birds safe from harm.

Suddenly! The children all started running up the bank and into the woods, hiding behind the trees and bushes. They all knew that to get flogged with those huge wings, or pinched by the big gander would be very painful.

Although Jeremy couldn't hear them, it was plain to see they were excited by the way that they were running and waving their arms. Then he saw the reason why. Not ten feet behind the children was the big gander! His wings were spread to their fullest width and flapping wildly. His neck was stretched way out, and his mouth was open. Jeremy had no doubt the bird was angry and neither did the children that had been teasing him.

When the children had disappeared into the woods, the gander looked around to see if the danger was gone. After he was satisfied his geese were safe, he walked back to the water's edge, and taking one last look around, slid ever so gracefully back into the water. Jeremy watched as the gander swam around the geese, checking each one to see if they had been harmed before taking up his position between them and the edge of the pond. The big gander swam back and forth for a while and then settled himself in a sunny spot on the pond and began to preen his feathers.

Oh! What a beautiful site he was cleaning and sunning himself out there on that pond. Every once in a while he would move his long neck forward and dip his beak into the water and then go back to working on his feathers. It made Jeremy think of when he dipped his hands into the water when he was cleaning himself up at home.

Just then the geese swam into a little inlet not thirty feet from where he was hiding. He wanted to get a better look at the big gander and his geese, but to do that he had to get closer. Very quietly he slipped out from behind his tree and walked ever so slowly down to the water's edge. As he moved along he could see the big gander watching him. The big birds' head raised up and turned slowly watching as Jeremy moved closer and closer to the water's edge. The gander was in no mood for more foolishness today and began to move slowly toward where Jeremy was heading.

Jeremy sat down at the water's edge and smiled as the big gander got closer and closer. "He is very beautiful," he thought to himself as he watched the big bird.

Now, Jeremy knew very well that big old gander could be mean so he sat very carefully on the grass next to the water to watch.

All at once, that big gander stretched his neck way out and HISSSSSSSSED a warning at Jeremy to leave his pond.

Of course Jeremy did not know the big bird had made such a terrible sound because his world was very quiet. Jeremy saw that big old gander turn in the water then spread out his big wings and his long neck and start to swim ever so gracefully toward him.

His little heart leaped with excitement and joy when this giant goose came out of the water and up the bank. When the gander got close, Jeremy reached out his hand to touch the big bird. In that instant that old gander pinched his little fingers so hard he thought he had lost them. He couldn't know it, but there was laughter and shouting from the other side of the pond where the other children were watching.

Jeremy jerked his hand back and with tears running down his cheeks ran all the way back to the stone fence his father had built around their little cottage. He dare not go in because he knew his mother would never let him go exploring again. She was afraid he would get into trouble in the forest and could not call for help. If that happened, they would never see Jeremy again.

Jeremy waited there by the stone fence until suppertime, then he dried his eyes and straightened his cap and went inside.

The children of the village had thought it great fun to watch as Jeremy tried to make friends with that old gander. They had been teasing that goose for years and knew he wasn't going to let anyone even get close. Especially this boy who couldn't talk or hear! It was decided they would watch him and see what happened next. So they all got up very early and went back to hide in the woods and watch.

The very next morning Jeremy got up, dressed and ate his breakfast as usual. His mother put his coat on him and sent him outside to play. He looked back to see if anyone was watching before he slipped back into the forest and headed for the pond. He sat behind a tree and watched the big geese swim around and around the lily pond, and always the big gander would swim along behind them.

Jeremy waited until all the geese were at the far end of the pond. Then he stepped out from behind the tree and moved very carefully down to the water's edge and sat down on the grass next to the pond.

Well, that big gander saw Jeremy and headed straight for the spot where he was setting. He spread his huge wings and stretched his long neck and began HISSSSSSSSING and splashing water, and coming very fast! He got there only to find Jeremy had gone, but where he had been there were three large crumbs of bread. The big gander gobbled these up and looked for more before he went back into the pond.

The children across the way saw little Jeremy jump up and run away into the woods. It was very funny to them and they laughed and laughed.

For three days Jeremy did this and each day the big gander was a little slower about trying to drive him away. Each day the big gander would spend more and more time looking for the crumbs that might have been left behind.

On the fourth day as Jeremy made his way through the forest, he had a very serious look on his face. He stopped just behind the tree that was nearest to the pond and peeked carefully around it to find out where the big gander was. When Jeremy saw him on the other side of the pond, he very carefully went over and sat down to wait.

Today Jeremy thought he was ready for the giant bird. He sat there with his coat on and the collar pulled way up around his neck. He had pulled his hat down over his ears in case the gander wanted to pinch them. His mother had pinched his ear once when he was bad and he knew that hurt very badly.

It was possible that this big bird might just pull one of them off, if he got a good hold on it. Jeremy could not hear but he did want both his ears.

He had his little hands squeezed into fists and pulled up inside his coat sleeves. His eyes were squinted shut so he could just barely see out of them. He was scrunched down to where he almost looked more like a tree stump than a little boy.

As Jeremy sat there waiting, he could see the big goose looking his way. The big bird stretched out his long neck and his big wings and started to swim across the pond toward him. He could see the goose looked angry and that he was making sounds. All Jeremy could hear was his heart beating with excitement as he sat there waiting for whatever was going to happen next.

"Well now. What was this that was setting on the grass next to the water? It did not look like that little boy that has been bringing those wonderful tasting crumbs. I will see what it is."

Jeremy could see the goose coming closer. But he did not come right out of the water as before. Instead he swam back and forth, back and forth. Looking to see if that thing setting on the grass was a danger to him and his geese.

The children watching from the other side of the pond became very quiet. What was Jeremy doing? That gander was almost as big as Jeremy and they all knew if that big bird got him down and started flogging him and pinching him, he would be hurt very badly before he could get away! They all held their breath and watched.

The gander came out of the water and slowly waddled over to where Jeremy was setting. The big bird walked all the way around Jeremy, touching him here and there on the coat and hat. Little Jeremy's heart was beating very fast but he didn't move a muscle. He just sat there squinting out of his little eyes.

The big goose walked around and around. Finally he stopped right in front of Jeremy. He moved his head back and forth very slowly looking at the little boy.

As the big bird stood towering over him, Jeremy very slowly began to push his fist out the end of his coat sleeve. He slowly held out his hand and turned it over. As the giant bird stood looking at Jeremy, he opened his fists and there were four large crumbs of bread.

The big gander slowly lowered his head and ever so gently picked them out of his hand one at a time. After the crumbs were gone, the big goose stood looking at Jeremy all scrunched down and squinting. Jeremy opened his eyes and at once the gander recognized him. Still, he did not move.

"Why, this is my little boy after all!"

Jeremy smiled at the big gander and slowly reached his hand out and let it come to rest where the long neck joined the big body of the goose.

The children watching from across the pond looked on in wonderment. This little boy, who could neither talk nor hear, had done something no one else in the village had been able to do. He had made friends with this goose. Could it be that he was just a little bit special? Could it be they might actually learn something from someone who was different from them? A lesson had been learned that would not be forgotten. Perhaps we could all learn from this same lesson.

What we learned.

When Jeremy reached out and touched the goose it was as if something magic had happened. In that moment the love flowed from that little hand resting on the neck of that giant gander and made a bond of friendship that would last forever.

That old gander just sat right down at Jeremy's feet and the rest of the morning was spent just being friends.

It was quiet there. The morning sun was shining down on that little forest clearing. A very special little boy had made a friend out of one of nature's most beautiful creatures, and that friendship would last forever.

As Jeremy grew older, he discovered it was not necessary to be like everyone else to be happy. From that time on he began to find other things to do. When we think about it, we are all different from each other in some way. Not being like everyone else is not so bad after all

☺

Made in the USA
Columbia, SC
12 September 2020